Ardmore

HOW DO YOU WRAP A HORSE?

BY DIANA KLEMIN

Watercolors by

CHRIS L. DEMAREST

GUILDAMERICA
B O O K S

DOUBLEDAY BOOK & MUSIC CLUBS, INC. GARDEN CITY, NEW YORK

To Charles Augustus de Kay
who asked the question
— D. K.

For Cara, Eliza and Dana
— C. D.

CHARLES OPENED THE FRONT DOOR just in time to see his mom tuck odd-sized boxes into the hall closet. It's almost Christmas, he reminded himself.

Charles went into the kitchen where his sister, Jennie, was fixing a snack. "What do you think we should give Mom and Dad for Christmas?" Charles whispered.

Jennie thought a minute. "How about a cordless screwdriver for Dad and a plant for Mom?"

"That's a boring present for Mom," Charles said. "What she really wants is a horse. She told me this summer that she had a pony once, and she'd like to ride again. And we have room for a horse—the garden shed was once a stable, remember?"

Jennie laughed. "We don't have the money to buy a horse! But maybe we could paint a picture of one and frame it."

Charles liked the idea, so they took wrapping paper and Magic Markers to the attic where they'd have lots of room to work and their mom wouldn't see them.

Charles drew the horse's head and legs and painted them brown. Jennie painted a gray body and tail. When they finished, Charles stood back to have a good look.

"That's not a horse—that's a freak! Who ever saw a horse with a brown head and a dapple-gray body?"

"You're right, " Jennie said. "We can make a better horse than that."

They took fresh paper, and with black paint only, they drew carefully all afternoon.

Finally, Charles shook his head. "This painting is terrible. The horse's neck is as long as a giraffe's and its legs are as short as a pony's. Mom would laugh."

Wearily, they packed up their paints, rolled up the paintings, and went downstairs.

"Maybe we could buy a horse after all," Jennie said. "Let's look in the newspaper."

Charles found the Sunday paper. There were golden retriever puppies for sale, free kittens, a pony for hire and, finally:

> GENTLE HORSE NEEDS KIND HOME.
> OWNER MOVING TO CITY.
> PRICE REASONABLE. 24 SKY LANE.

"That's the horse for Mom. Let's skip karate lessons tomorrow and buy it."

When they got home from school the next day Mom was out, so Jennie emptied both piggy banks and found eighty-three dollars and thirty cents.

Charles filled his pockets with sugar cubes. Everyone knows that horses love sugar.

Jumping on their bikes, they pedaled way out in the back country to 24 Sky Lane. Charles rang the bell. He was nervous. Would eighty-three dollars and thirty cents be enough money?

A lady opened the door. "Hello, can I help you?"

"I am Charles East and this is my sister, Jennie. We've come to buy your horse. We're going to give it to our mother for Christmas. Is eighty-three dollars and thirty cents enough?"

"I'm Mrs. Perry. I know your parents," the lady said, looking at the children closely. "Won't you come into the kitchen for milk and cookies. There are questions I would like to ask. First of all, can you handle a horse? And do you have a stable?"

"I rode a horse at camp," Charles said. "And we help our neighbors with their horses."

"We have a big garden shed that was once a stable," Jennie chimed in. "We will feed and groom the horse every day before and after school."

"Does your dad know you are giving your mom a horse?" asked Mrs. Perry.

Charles looked at Jennie for support. "Not exactly, but as long as we take care of it, Dad won't mind. He knows Mom wants a horse."

Mrs. Perry said solemnly, "Adopting a horse is a big responsibility. Do you know that it costs a lot of money to feed a horse and pay the vet bills? How are you going to manage?"

"I earn money baby-sitting, Charles has a paper route, and we both make money cleaning the neighbor's horse stalls," Jennie answered.

Mrs. Perry smiled. "Come, let's visit my Daisy in the barn and see how the three of you get along."

Daisy whinnied softly at her stall door. Then she nuzzled in Charles's pocket and found the sugar.

Charles jumped with joy. "She is just the color brown Mom likes!" He saddled Daisy and led her from the barn. Then he took the reins and climbed into the saddle. Jennie sat bareback behind Charles. He tapped Daisy on her rump. Off she trotted across the snow-covered meadow. Gently he pulled the left rein. Daisy slowed down and turned back to the barn.

"Charles, you ride well," said Mrs. Perry.

He took off the saddle, hung it on its peg, and rubbed Daisy down. Jennie gave her a bag of feed and put a blanket on her for the night.

"Is eighty-three dollars and thirty cents enough?" Charles repeated.

"I was asking much more money," said Mrs. Perry. "However, what is more important is that Daisy have the right home. Since you are kind children who know how to handle a horse, I accept your offer—on one condition. If your parents object to Daisy, I'll take her back. Okay?"

"Oh yes!" both children said at once.

"Good. When will you come for her?" asked Mrs. Perry.

"We'll be here at five on Christmas Eve," Jennie said.

As they said goodbye to Daisy, she took another sugar from Charles's pocket.

The following Saturday the children swept the garden shed, making it a clean stable for Daisy. Their mother was amazed when she saw them on ladders, washing the windows, and hosing down the hay bins.

"I can't believe my eyes!" she cried. "What's gotten into you two?"

"Dad promised to give us twenty dollars if we cleaned out the shed."

"Whatever for?" she asked them. "You aren't bringing home a horse, are you?" The children looked at each other, stunned. Then they went on cleaning.

Christmas Eve finally came.

In the living room, Charles and Jennie were hanging the ornaments on the tree when Charles looked out the window. "It's snowing. It might be a blizzard! Let's get Daisy now." Telling their mom they were going to play in the snow, they put on boots and windbreakers and set out on foot to collect Daisy.

Arriving at the farm, they met Mrs, Perry at the door. "You can't ride Daisy home in a snowstorm," she said. "Daisy would slip, and you might fall off. Wait until the storm is over and the roads are plowed."

Silently they trudged home. They were very disappointed.

"Where have you been?" their dad called as they slipped into the house. "Do you know it is after seven o'clock? We were worried."

"Sorry, Dad. We didn't realize how late it was."

"Well," he said, "it's time for supper and then I'll read A Christmas Carol before you go to bed."

On Christmas morning Charles and Jennie woke up early. It was quiet and cold. The snow was deep. "The road hasn't been plowed," moaned Charles. "There's no hope of getting Daisy today. And it won't be Christmas without a present for Mom."

"We'll give Mom a card, saying a present will arrive when the road is plowed," said Jennie.

Just then they heard a crunching on the snow.

"Look!" Charles shouted. "It's Mrs. Perry bringing Daisy in a U-Haul!" They raced outside.

"I couldn't sleep a wink. I had to deliver your mom's present," said Mrs. Perry as she led Daisy to the stable. Jennie hung up her saddle and tack. Charles carted the hay and feed from the U-Haul.

"Daisy, I love you," Mrs. Perry told her. "I wish I didn't have to leave you, but you wouldn't like living in the city. So be a good horse in your new home." Mrs. Perry kissed Daisy goodbye.

She turned to Jennie and Charles. "Remember what I told you. If your parents refuse to keep Daisy, I'll come for her in the morning."

When she had gone Charles said, "A Christmas present has to be wrapped. How do you wrap a horse?"

"With Christmas paper, of course," said Jennie.

Quietly, so as not to wake their parents, Charles and Jennie went back to the house. They brought out all the Christmas paper they could carry. They taped rolls and rolls of paper over Daisy's blanket.

"You're not doing it neatly," Jennie scolded.

"Yes I am," answered Charles. "But it's hard to wrap a moving package!" Just then, Daisy shook her mane and kicked her front hoof through the paper.

So they taped more paper over the hole.

Then they made paper leggings and tied them around each leg.

"Jennie, tie the big bow on her tail," Charles directed.

"No, that bow is for the card," Jennie responded.

"A horse can have several bows," said Charles as he tied one on her tail.

Jennie hung the big bow with the card around Daisy's neck:

MERRY CHRISTMAS TO MOM
YOUR OWN HORSE
WITH LOVE, CHARLES AND JENNIE

Last, they made a hood for her head and mane. Only her ears and eyes could be seen.

Daisy was completely wrapped and getting restless. She snorted and twitched her tail.

"Let's call Mom and Dad right now," said Charles.

When Mr. East saw the parcel, he groaned. "What is this?"

Daisy whinnied loudly.

Mr. East gasped. "Oh, no! Not a horse! I've slept with a cat and I've slept with a dog, and I will not sleep with a horse. Never! Take her back where she came from this instant."

"Oh, she's wonderful!" said Mrs. East.

Mrs. East took off Daisy's hood and hugged the children to her side. "Thank you for the best Christmas present I ever received."

Mr. East stroked Daisy's forehead. "Well," he said. "Since your mother likes her so much and if you two promise to take care of her, maybe we can keep her."

Charles and Jennie beamed. Then and there they knew that Daisy could stay.

So they all had hot chocolate and muffins for Christmas breakfast while Daisy had some oats with her mash.

And Mr. East unwrapped and tried his cordless screwdriver.